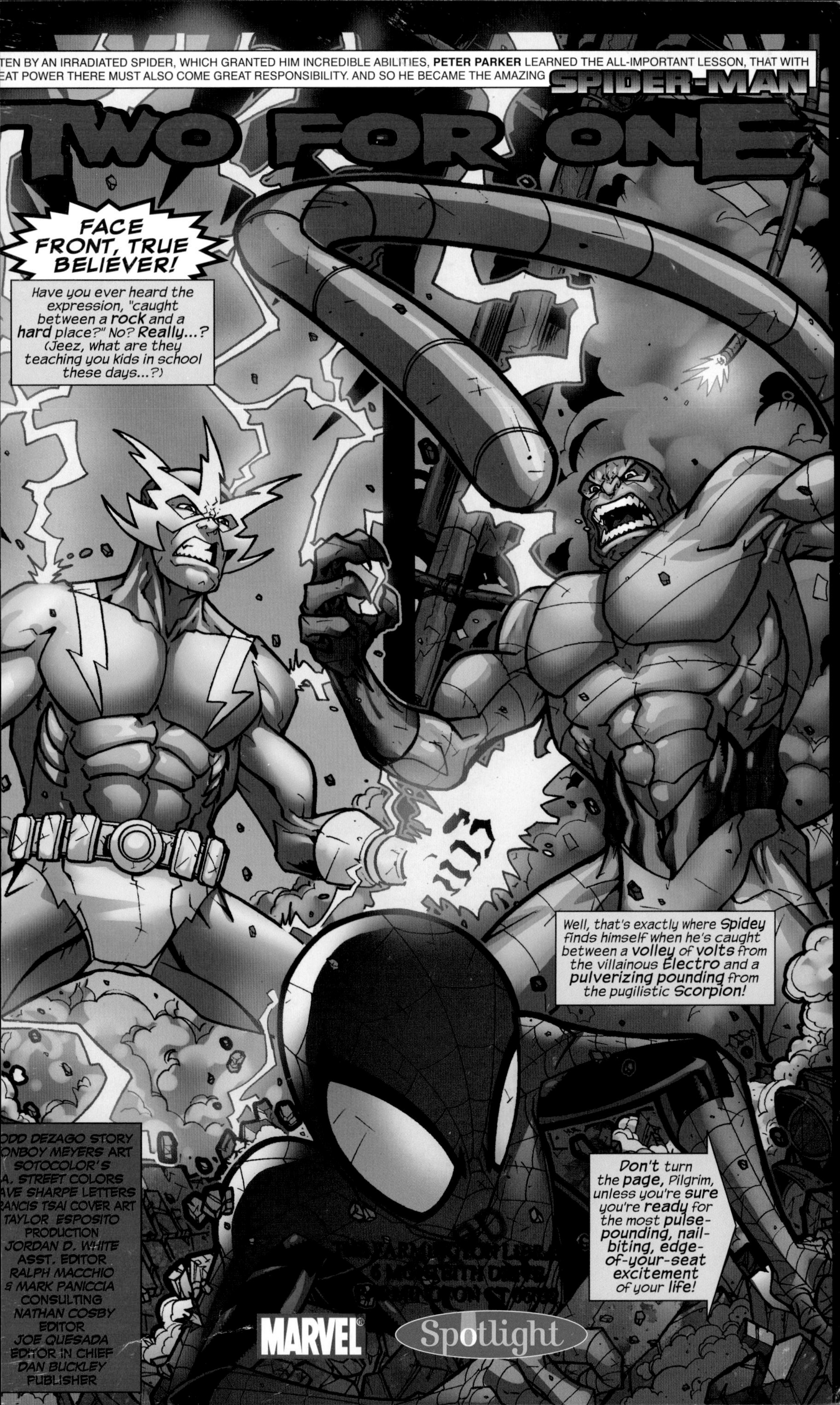

TEN BY AN IRRADIATED SPIDER, WHICH GRANTED HIM INCREDIBLE ABILITIES, PETER PARKER LEARNED THE ALL-IMPORTANT LESSON, THAT WITH EAT POWER THERE MUST ALSO COME GREAT RESPONSIBILITY. AND SO HE BECAME THE AMAZING SPIDER-MAN
TWO FOR ONE
FACE FRONT, TRUE BELIEVER!
Have you ever heard the expression, "caught between a rock and a hard place?" No? Really...? (Jeez, what are they teaching you kids in school these days...?)
Well, that's exactly where Spidey finds himself when he's caught between a volley of volts from the villainous Electro and a pulverizing pounding from the pugilistic Scorpion!
ODD DEZAGO STORY
ONBOY MEYERS ART
SOTOCOLOR'S
A. STREET COLORS
AVE SHARPE LETTERS
RANCIS TSAI COVER ART
TAYLOR ESPOSITO PRODUCTION
JORDAN D. WHITE ASST. EDITOR
RALPH MACCHIO & MARK PANICCIA CONSULTING
NATHAN COSBY EDITOR
JOE QUESADA EDITOR IN CHIEF
DAN BUCKLEY PUBLISHER
Don't turn the page, Pilgrim, unless you're sure you're ready for the most pulse-pounding, nail-biting, edge-of-your-seat excitement of your life!
MARVEL
Spotlight

VISIT US AT
www.abdopublishing.com

Reinforced library bound edition published in 2011 by Spotlight, a division of the ABDO Group, 8000 West 78th Street, Edina, Minnesota 55439. Spotlight produces high-quality reinforced library bound editions for schools and libraries. Published by agreement with Marvel Characters, Inc.

Printed in the United States of America, Melrose Park, Illinois.
042010
092010
This book contains at least 10% recycled material.

Library of Congress Cataloging-in-Publication Data

Dezago, Todd.
 Two for one / story, Todd DeZago ; art, Jonboy Meyers. -- Reinforced library ed.
     p. cm. -- (Spider-Man (Series))
 "Marvel."
 Summary: Spider-Man faces off against both Scorpion and Electro, two nights in a row.
 ISBN 978-1-59961-779-4
 1. Graphic novels. [1. Graphic novels. 2. Superheroes--Fiction. 3. Robbers and outlaws--Fiction.] I. Meyers, Jonboy, ill. II. Title.
 PZ7.7.D508Two 2010
 741.5'973--dc22
                                   2009052843

All Spotlight books have reinforced library bindings and
are manufactured in the United States of America.

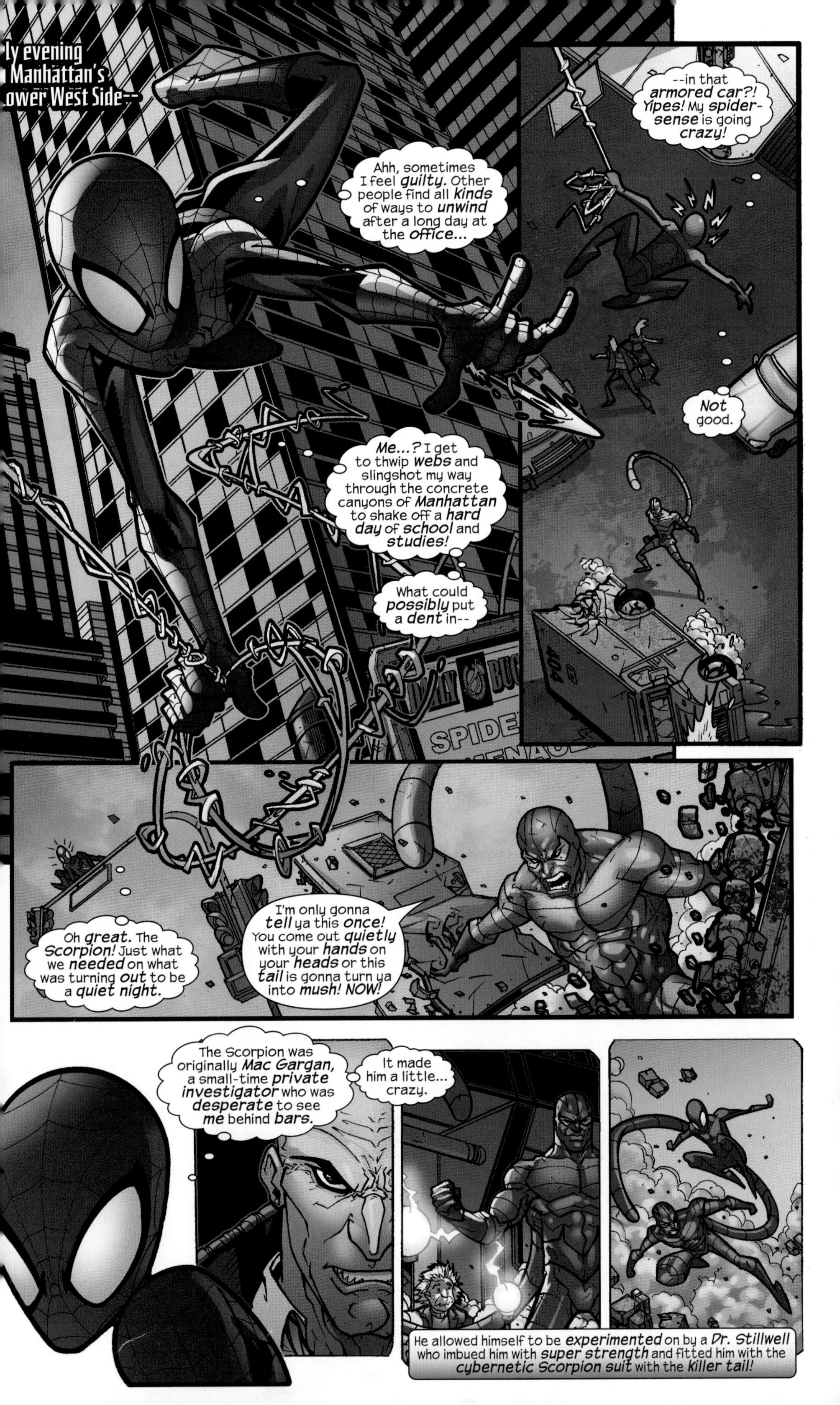
ly evening Manhattan's ower West Side--
Ahh, sometimes I feel guilty. Other people find all kinds of ways to unwind after a long day at the office...
Me...? I get to thwip webs and slingshot my way through the concrete canyons of Manhattan to shake off a hard day of school and studies!
What could possibly put a dent in--
--in that armored car?! Yipes! My spider-sense is going crazy!
Not good.
SPIDE
I'm only gonna tell ya this once! You come out quietly with your hands on your heads or this tail is gonna turn ya into mush! NOW!
Oh great. The Scorpion! Just what we needed on what was turning out to be a quiet night.
The Scorpion was originally Mac Gargan, a small-time private investigator who was desperate to see me behind bars.
It made him a little... crazy.
He allowed himself to be experimented on by a Dr. Stillwell who imbued him with super strength and fitted him with the cybernetic Scorpion suit with the killer tail!

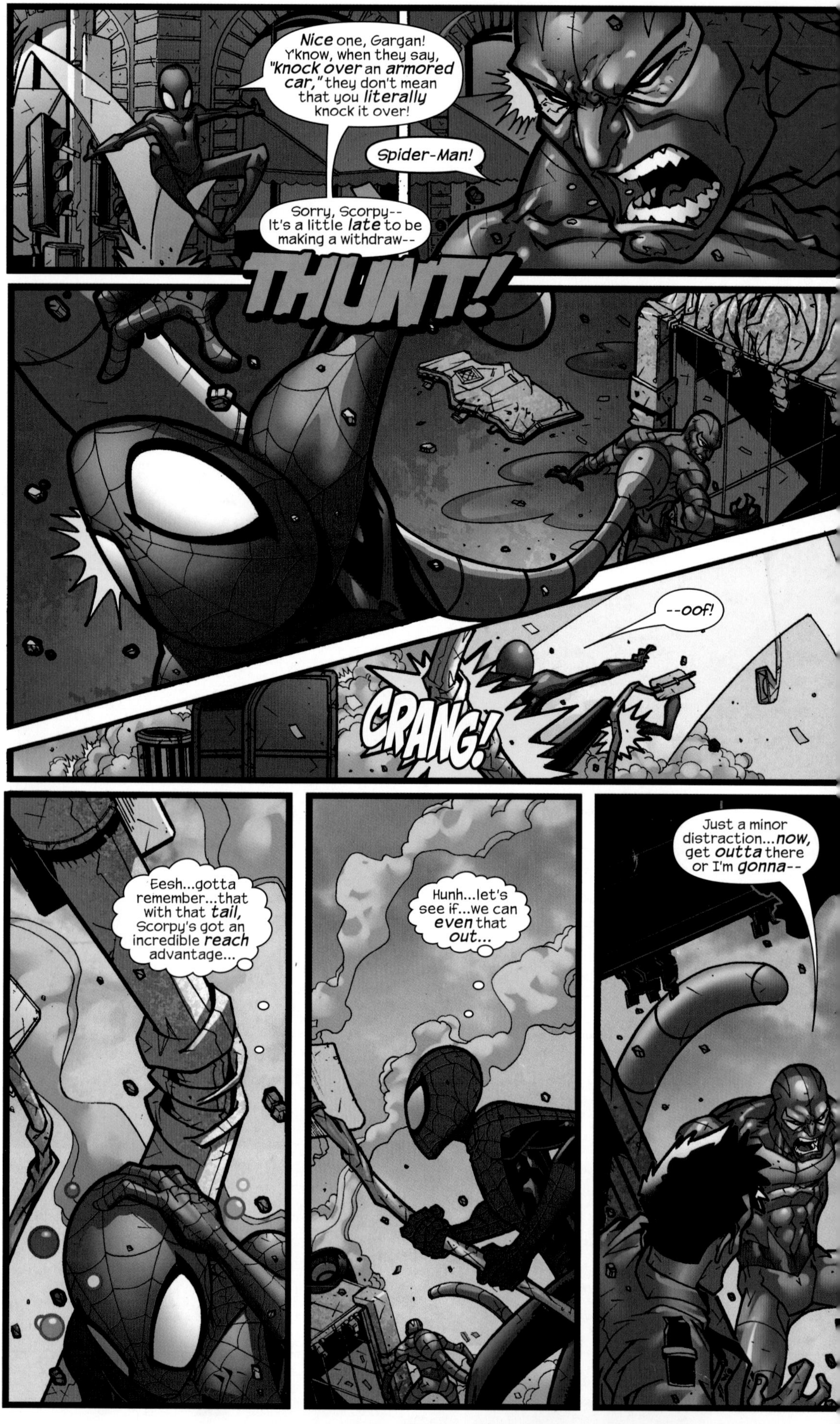

Nice one, Gargan! Y'know, when they say, "knock over an armored car," they don't mean that you literally knock it over!
Spider-Man!
Sorry, Scorpy-- It's a little late to be making a withdraw--
THUNT!
--oof!
CRANG!
Eesh...gotta remember...that with that tail, Scorpy's got an incredible reach advantage...
Hunh...let's see if...we can even that out...
Just a minor distraction...now, get outta there or I'm gonna--

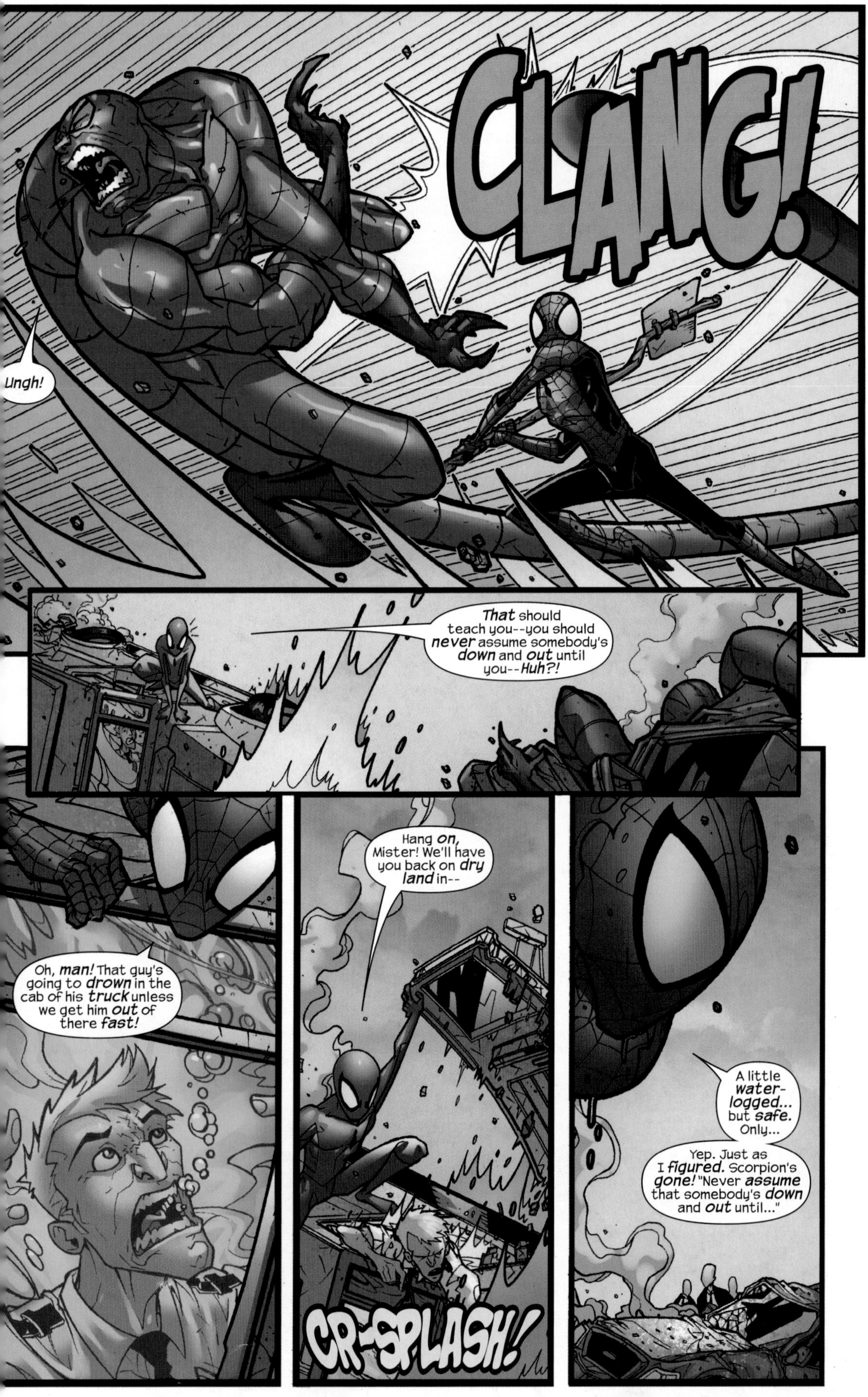
CLANG!
Ungh!
That should teach you--you should never assume somebody's down and out until you--Huh?!
Oh, man! That guy's going to drown in the cab of his truck unless we get him out of there fast!
Hang on, Mister! We'll have you back on dry land in--
CR-SPLASH!
A little water-logged... but safe. Only...
Yep. Just as I figured. Scorpion's gone! "Never assume that somebody's down and out until..."

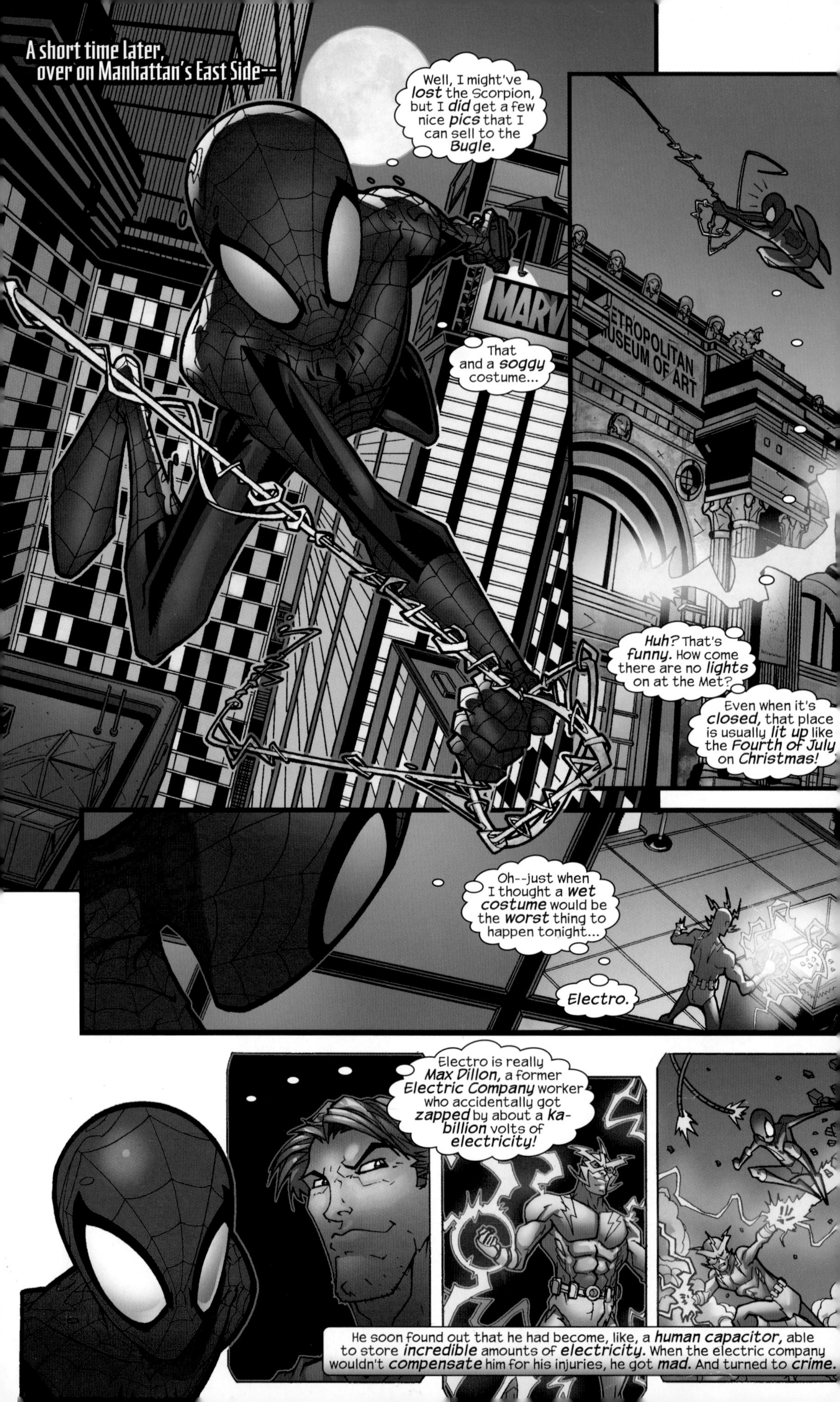

A short time later, over on Manhattan's East Side--
Well, I might've lost the Scorpion, but I did get a few nice pics that I can sell to the Bugle.
That and a soggy costume...
METROPOLITAN MUSEUM OF ART
Huh? That's funny. How come there are no lights on at the Met?
Even when it's closed, that place is usually lit up like the Fourth of July on Christmas!
Oh--just when I thought a wet costume would be the worst thing to happen tonight...
Electro.
Electro is really Max Dillon, a former Electric Company worker who accidentally got zapped by about a ka-billion volts of electricity!
He soon found out that he had become, like, a human capacitor, able to store incredible amounts of electricity. When the electric company wouldn't compensate him for his injuries, he got mad. And turned to crime.

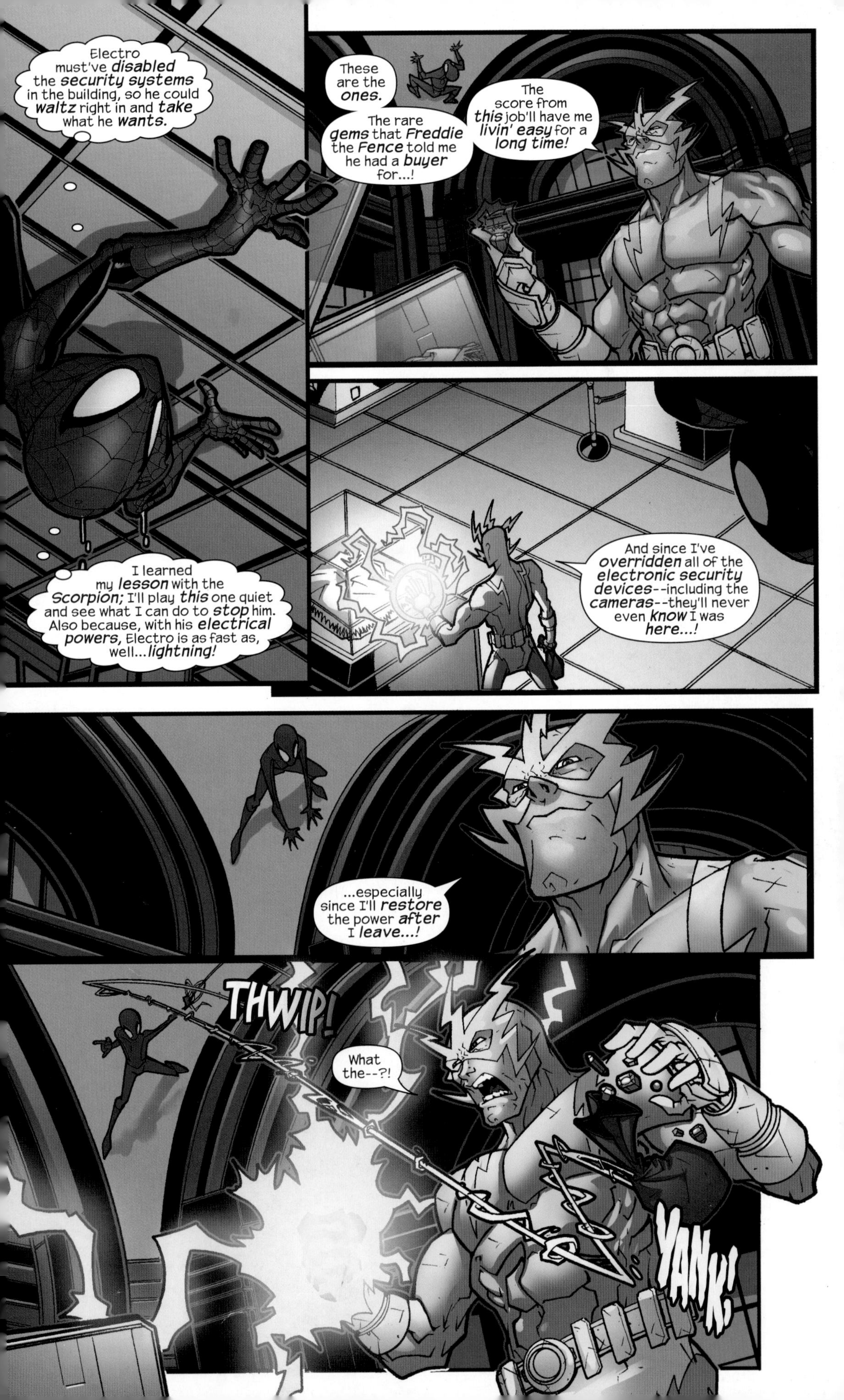
Electro must've disabled the security systems in the building, so he could waltz right in and take what he wants.
I learned my lesson with the Scorpion; I'll play this one quiet and see what I can do to stop him. Also because, with his electrical powers, Electro is as fast as, well...lightning!
These are the ones.
The rare gems that Freddie the Fence told me he had a buyer for...!
The score from this job'll have me livin' easy for a long time!
And since I've overridden all of the electronic security devices--including the cameras--they'll never even know I was here...!
...especially since I'll restore the power after I leave...!
THWIP!
What the--?!
YANK!

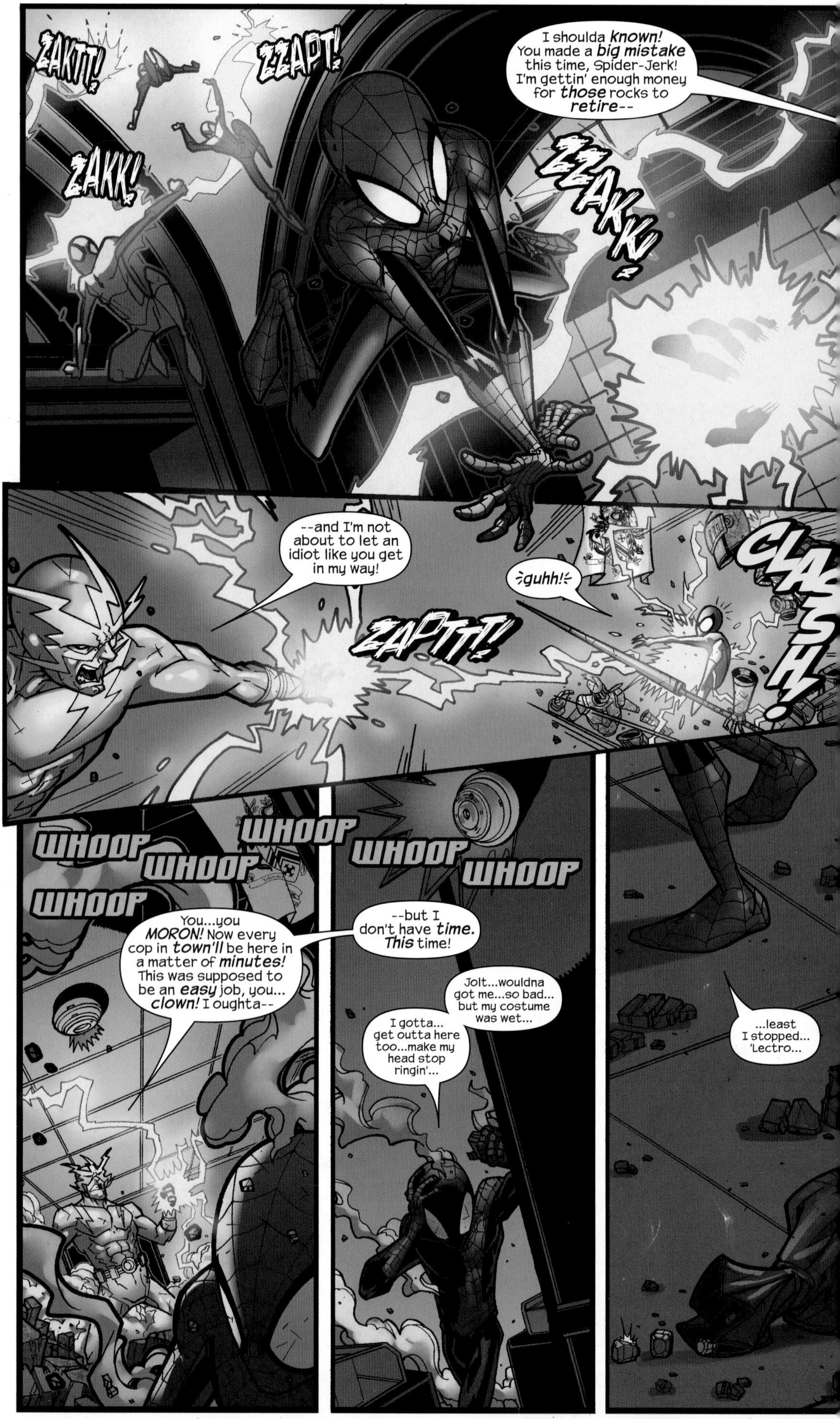

ZAKTT!
ZZAPT!
ZAKK!
I shoulda known! You made a big mistake this time, Spider-Jerk! I'm gettin' enough money for those rocks to retire--
ZZAKK!
--and I'm not about to let an idiot like you get in my way!
ZAPTTT!
guhh!
CLASSH!
WHOOP WHOOP WHOOP
WHOOP WHOOP WHOOP
You...you MORON! Now every cop in town'll be here in a matter of minutes! This was supposed to be an easy job, you... clown! I oughta--
--but I don't have time. This time!
Jolt...wouldna got me...so bad... but my costume was wet...
I gotta... get outta here too...make my head stop ringin'...
...least I stopped... 'Lectro...

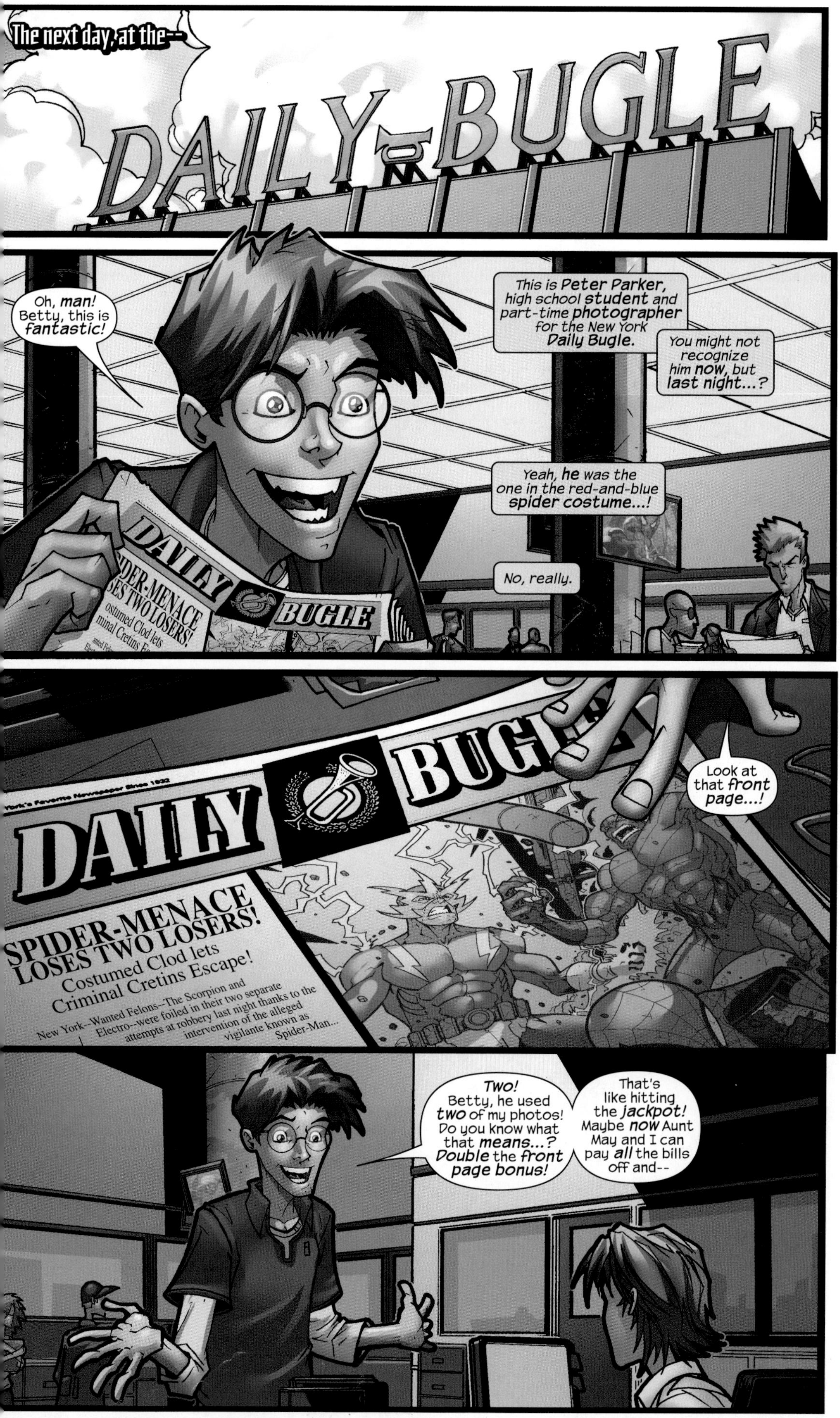

The next day, at the--
DAILY BUGLE
Oh, man! Betty, this is fantastic!
This is Peter Parker, high school student and part-time photographer for the New York Daily Bugle.
You might not recognize him now, but last night...?
Yeah, he was the one in the red-and-blue spider costume...!
No, really.
DAILY BUGLE
Look at that front page...!
SPIDER-MENACE LOSES TWO LOSERS!
Costumed Clod lets Criminal Cretins Escape!
New York--Wanted Felons--The Scorpion and Electro--were foiled in their two separate attempts at robbery last night thanks to the intervention of the alleged vigilante known as Spider-Man...
Two! Betty, he used two of my photos! Do you know what that means...? Double the front page bonus!
That's like hitting the jackpot! Maybe now Aunt May and I can pay all the bills off and--

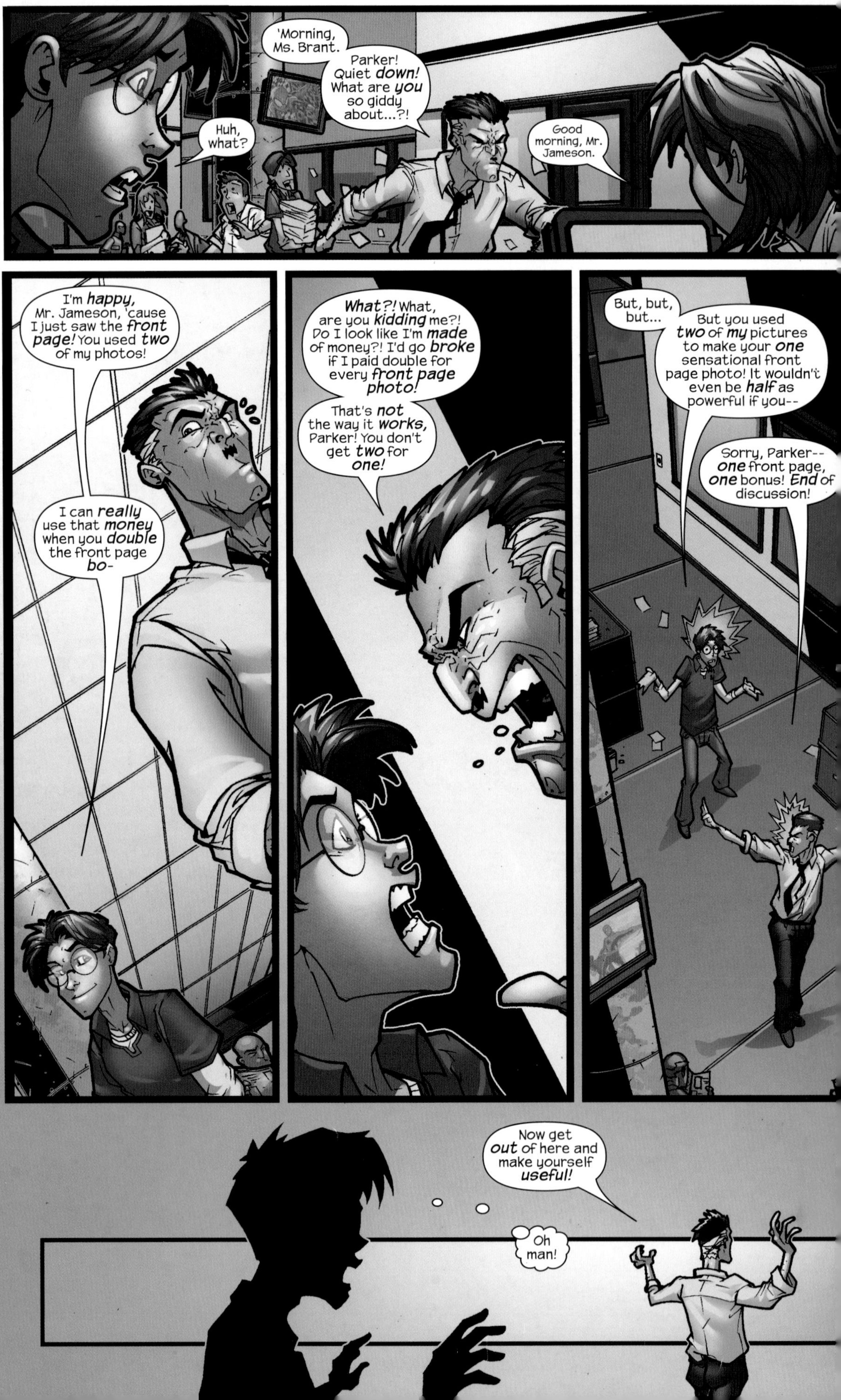

'Morning, Ms. Brant.
Parker! Quiet down! What are you so giddy about...?!
Huh, what?
Good morning, Mr. Jameson.
I'm happy, Mr. Jameson, 'cause I just saw the front page! You used two of my photos!
I can really use that money when you double the front page bo-
What?! What, are you kidding me?! Do I look like I'm made of money?! I'd go broke if I paid double for every front page photo!
That's not the way it works, Parker! You don't get two for one!
But, but, but...
But you used two of my pictures to make your one sensational front page photo! It wouldn't even be half as powerful if you--
Sorry, Parker-- one front page, one bonus! End of discussion!
Now get out of here and make yourself useful!
Oh man!

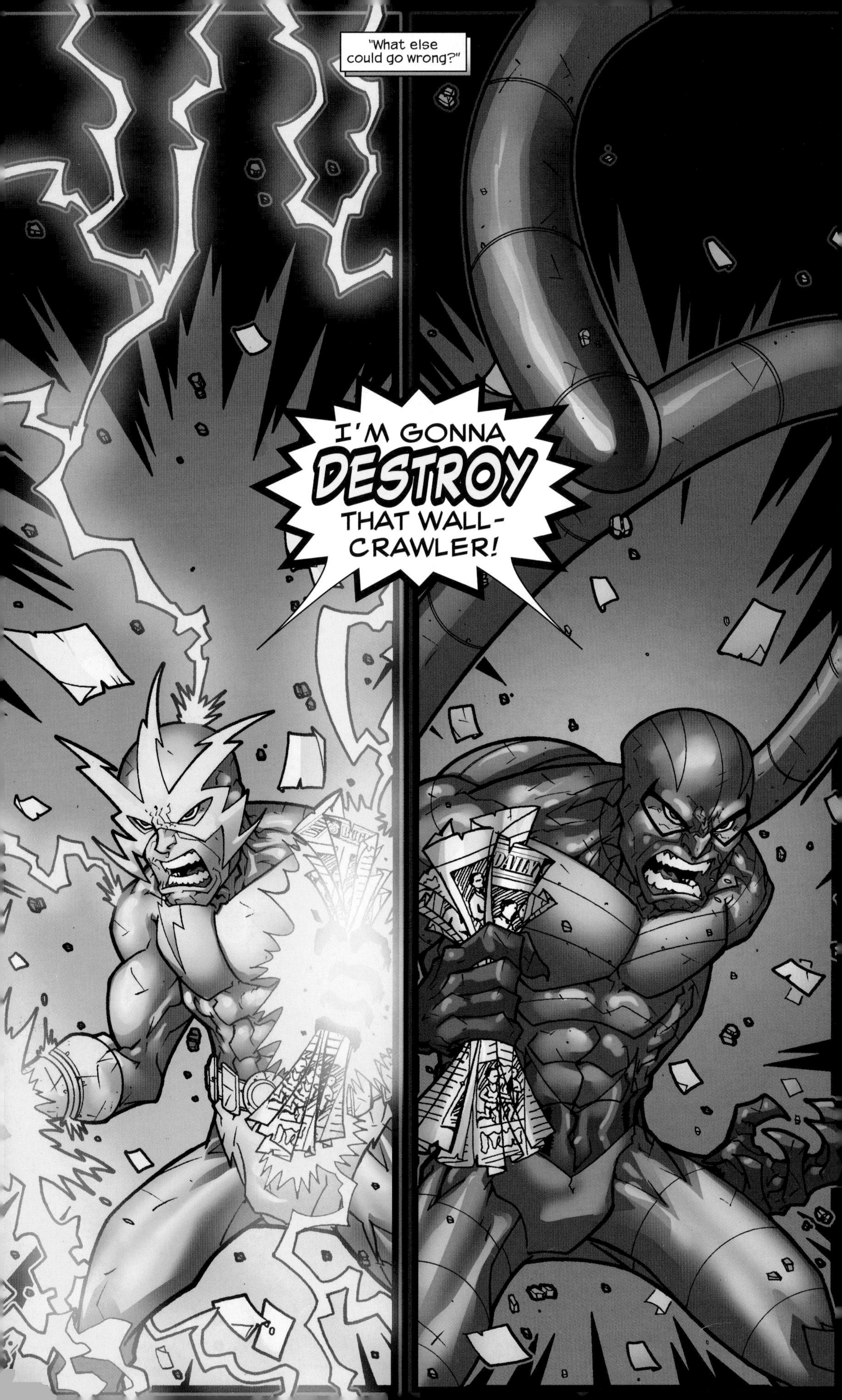
"What else could go wrong?"
I'M GONNA DESTROY THAT WALL-CRAWLER!

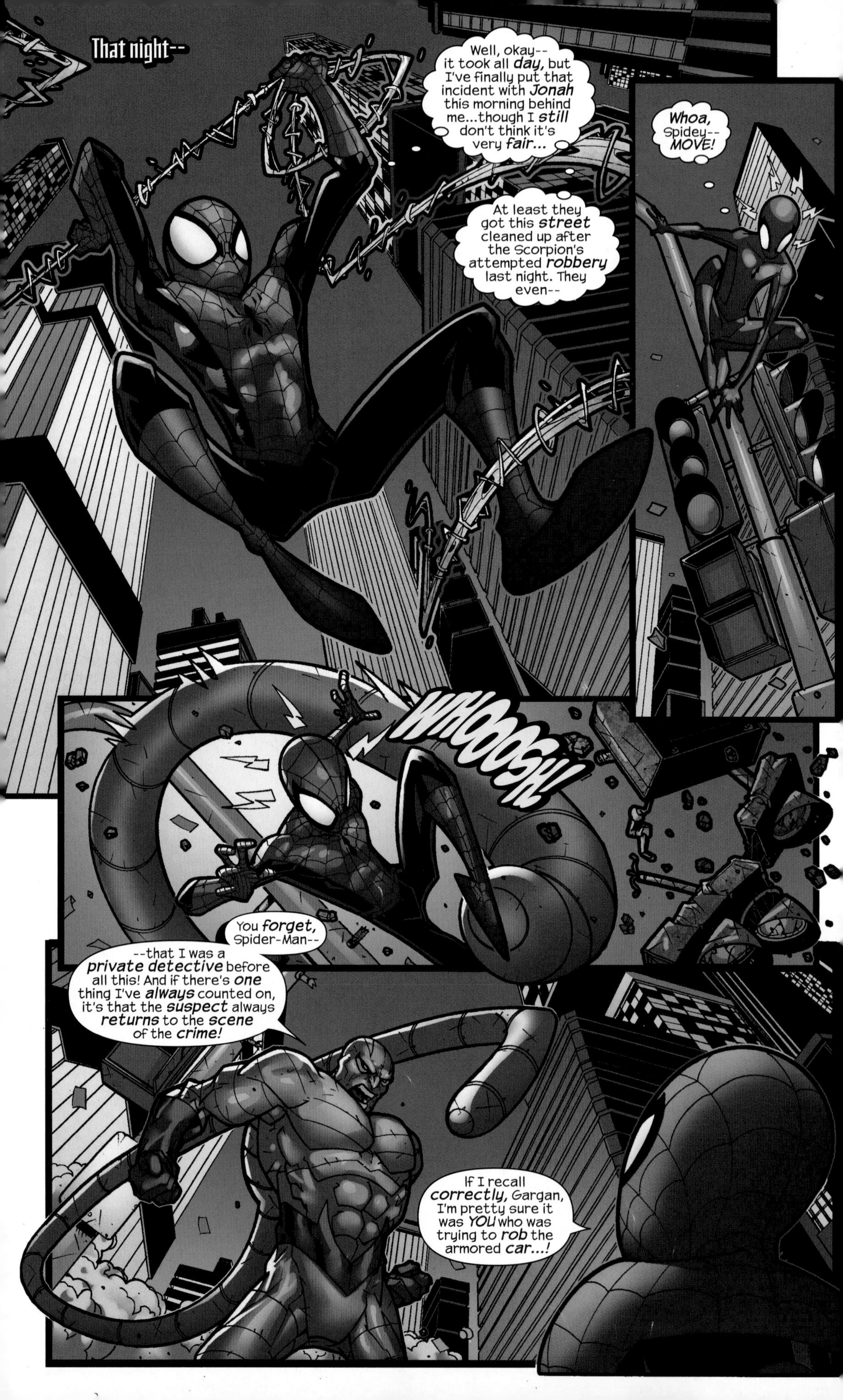
That night--
Well, okay-- it took all day, but I've finally put that incident with Jonah this morning behind me...though I still don't think it's very fair...
At least they got this street cleaned up after the Scorpion's attempted robbery last night. They even--
Whoa, Spidey-- MOVE!
WHOOOSH!
You forget, Spider-Man--
--that I was a private detective before all this! And if there's one thing I've always counted on, it's that the suspect always returns to the scene of the crime!
If I recall correctly, Gargan, I'm pretty sure it was YOU who was trying to rob the armored car...!

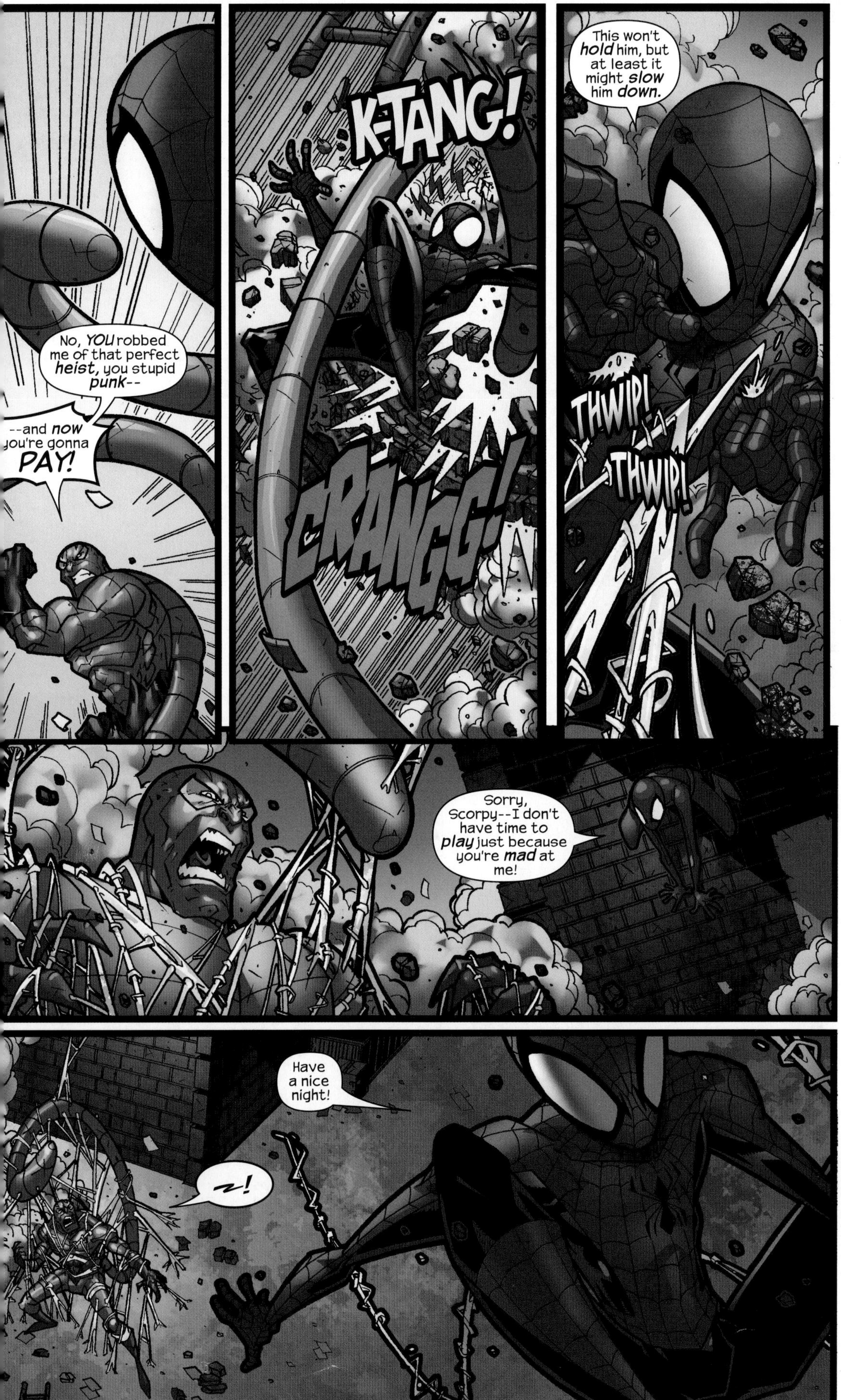
No, YOU robbed me of that perfect heist, you stupid punk--
--and now you're gonna PAY!
K-TANG!
CRANGG!
This won't hold him, but at least it might slow him down.
THWIP!
THWIP!
Sorry, Scorpy--I don't have time to play just because you're mad at me!
Have a nice night!
--!

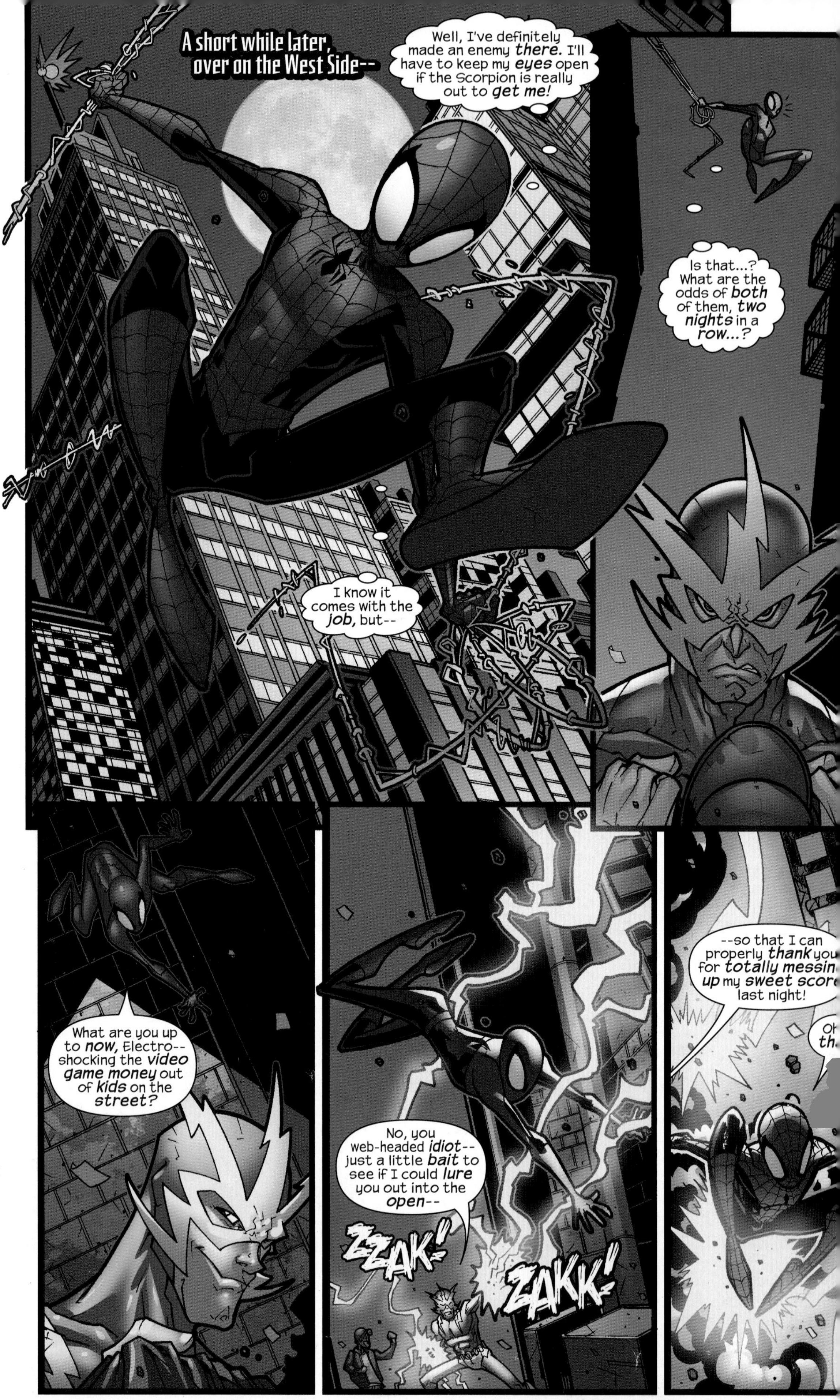
A short while later, over on the West Side--
Well, I've definitely made an enemy there. I'll have to keep my eyes open if the Scorpion is really out to get me!
I know it comes with the job, but--
Is that...? What are the odds of both of them, two nights in a row...?
What are you up to now, Electro--shocking the video game money out of kids on the street?
No, you web-headed idiot--just a little bait to see if I could lure you out into the open--
ZZZAK!
ZAKK!
--so that I can properly thank you for totally messin up my sweet score last night!

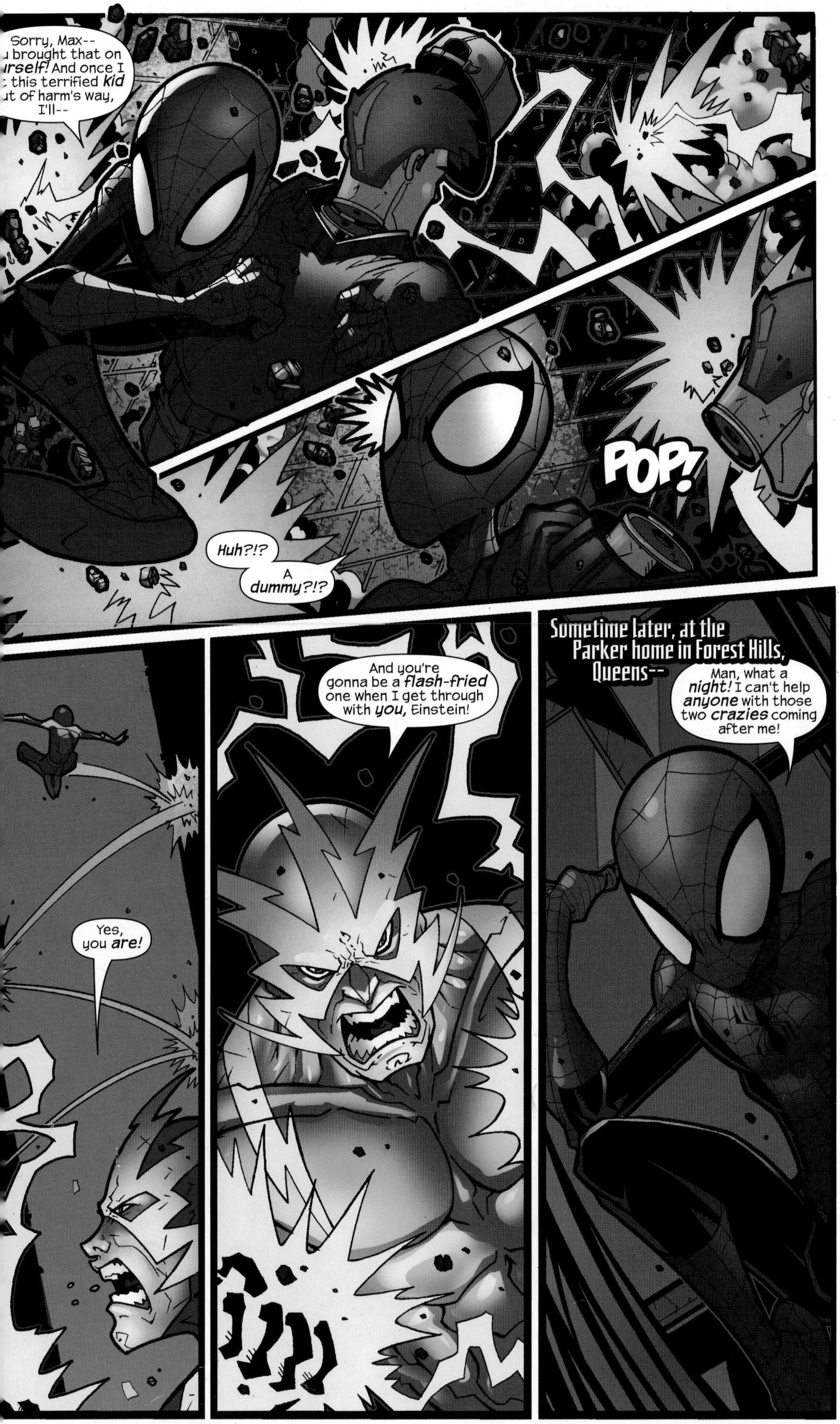
Sorry, Max-- u brought that on urself! And once I t this terrified kid ut of harm's way, I'll--
Huh?!?
A dummy?!?
POP!
Yes, you are!
And you're gonna be a flash-fried one when I get through with you, Einstein!
Sometime later, at the Parker home in Forest Hills, Queens--
Man, what a night! I can't help anyone with those two crazies coming after me!

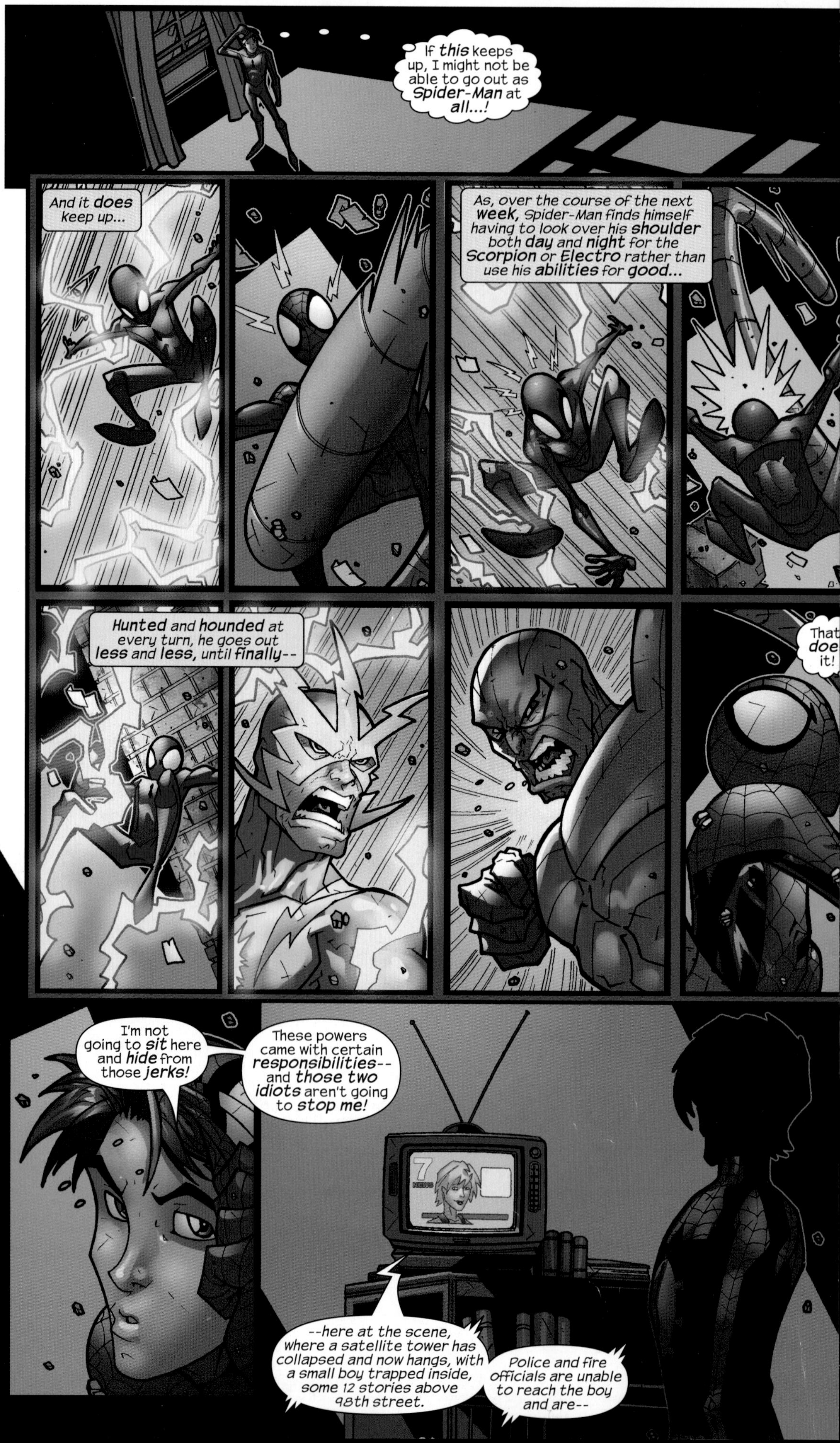

If this keeps up, I might not be able to go out as Spider-Man at all...!
And it does keep up...
As, over the course of the next week, Spider-Man finds himself having to look over his shoulder both day and night for the Scorpion or Electro rather than use his abilities for good...
Hunted and hounded at every turn, he goes out less and less, until finally--
That does it!
I'm not going to sit here and hide from those jerks!
These powers came with certain responsibilities--and those two idiots aren't going to stop me!
7 NEWS
--here at the scene, where a satellite tower has collapsed and now hangs, with a small boy trapped inside, some 12 stories above 98th street.
Police and fire officials are unable to reach the boy and are--

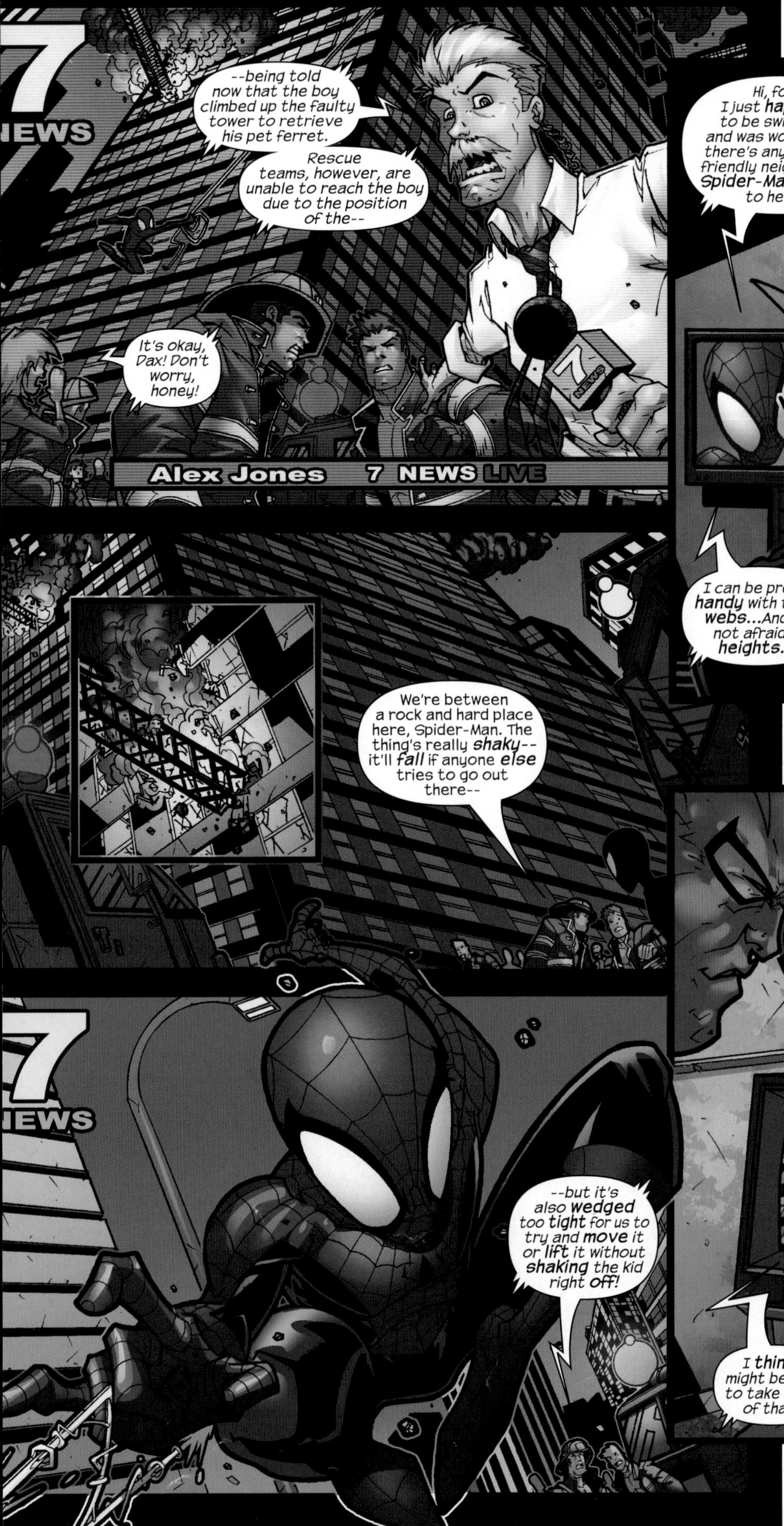
7 NEWS
--being told now that the boy climbed up the faulty tower to retrieve his pet ferret.
Rescue teams, however, are unable to reach the boy due to the position of the--
It's okay, Dax! Don't worry, honey!
Alex Jones 7 NEWS LIVE
Hi, folks! I just happened to be swinging by and was wondering if there's anything your friendly neighborhood Spider-Man might do to help...?
I can be pretty handy with these webs...And I'm not afraid of heights...!
We're between a rock and hard place here, Spider-Man. The thing's really shaky--it'll fall if anyone else tries to go out there--
7 NEWS
--but it's also wedged too tight for us to try and move it or lift it without shaking the kid right off!
I think I might be able to take care of that...

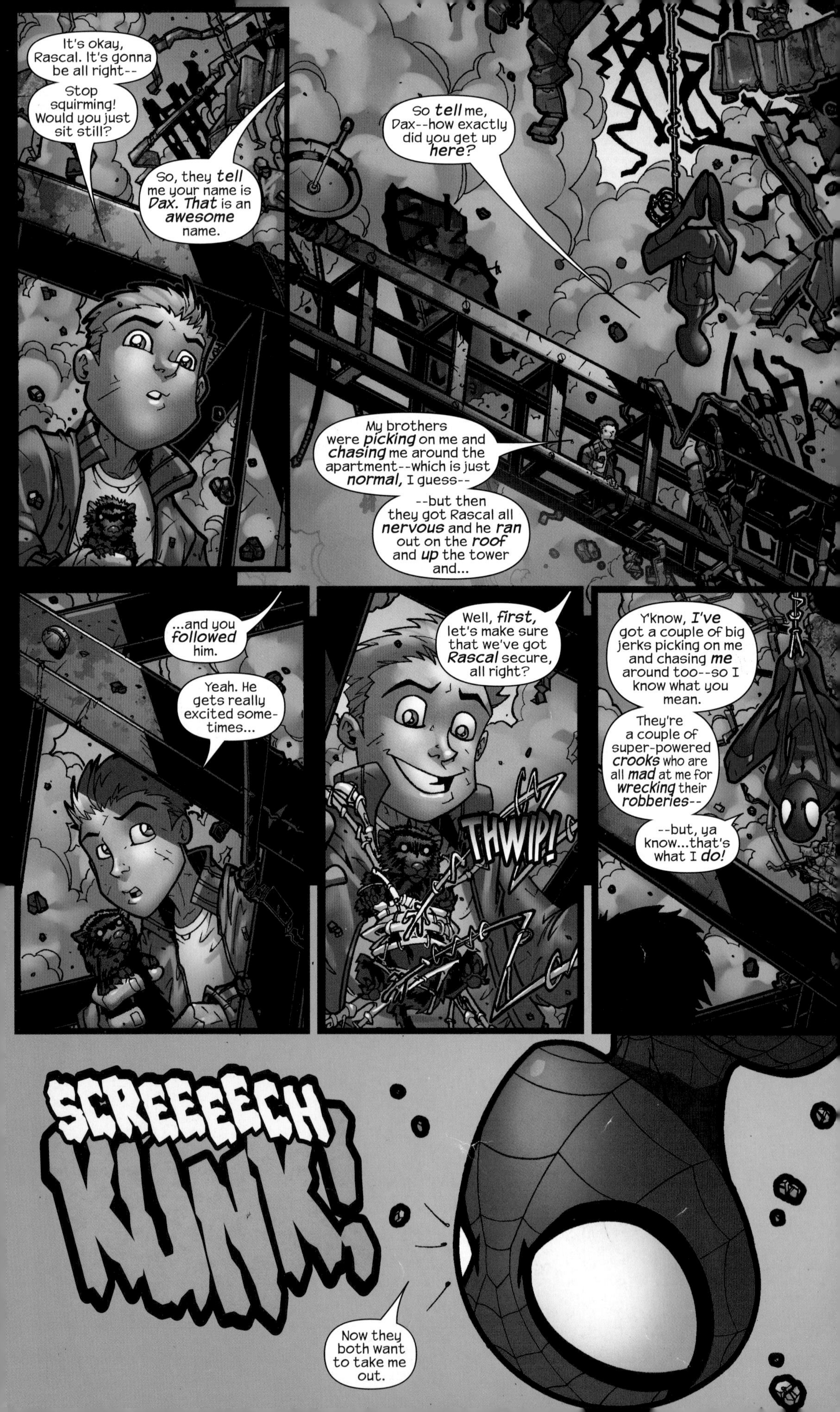

It's okay, Rascal. It's gonna be all right--
Stop squirming! Would you just sit still?
So, they *tell* me your name is *Dax. That* is an *awesome* name.
So *tell* me, Dax--how exactly did you get up *here?*
My brothers were *picking* on me and *chasing* me around the apartment--which is just *normal,* I guess--
--but then they got Rascal all *nervous* and he *ran* out on the *roof* and *up* the tower and...
...and you *followed* him.
Yeah. He gets really excited some-times...
Well, *first,* let's make sure that we've got *Rascal* secure, all right?
THWIP!
Y'know, *I've* got a couple of big jerks picking on me and chasing *me* around too--so I know what you mean.
They're a couple of super-powered *crooks* who are all *mad* at me for *wrecking* their *robberies*--
--but, ya know...that's what I *do!*
SCREEEECH
KUNK!
Now they both want to take me out.

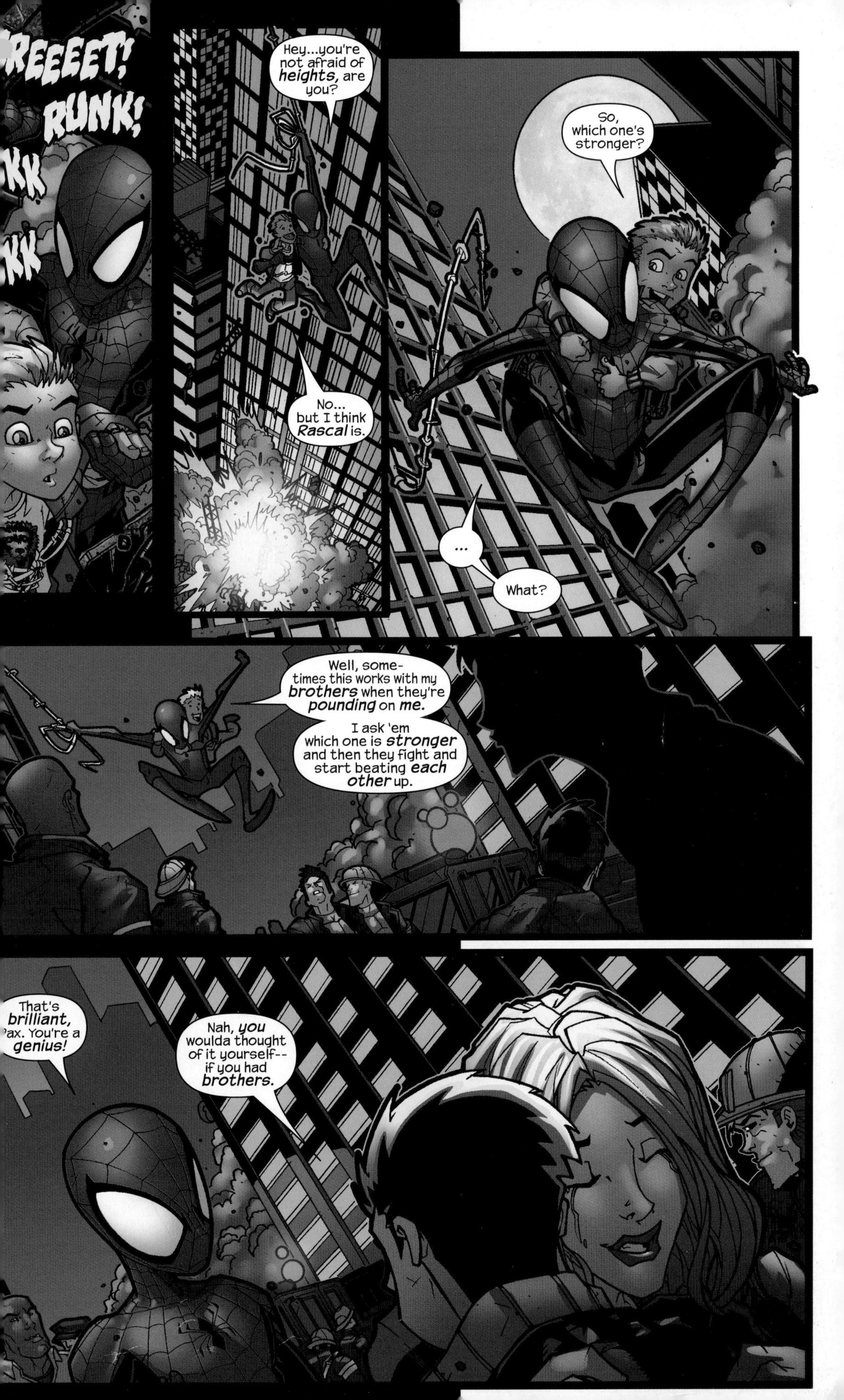

REEEET!
RUNK!
Hey...you're not afraid of heights, are you?
No... but I think Rascal is.
So, which one's stronger?
...
What?
Well, sometimes this works with my brothers when they're pounding on me.
I ask 'em which one is stronger and then they fight and start beating each other up.
That's brilliant, Pax. You're a genius!
Nah, you woulda thought of it yourself--if you had brothers.

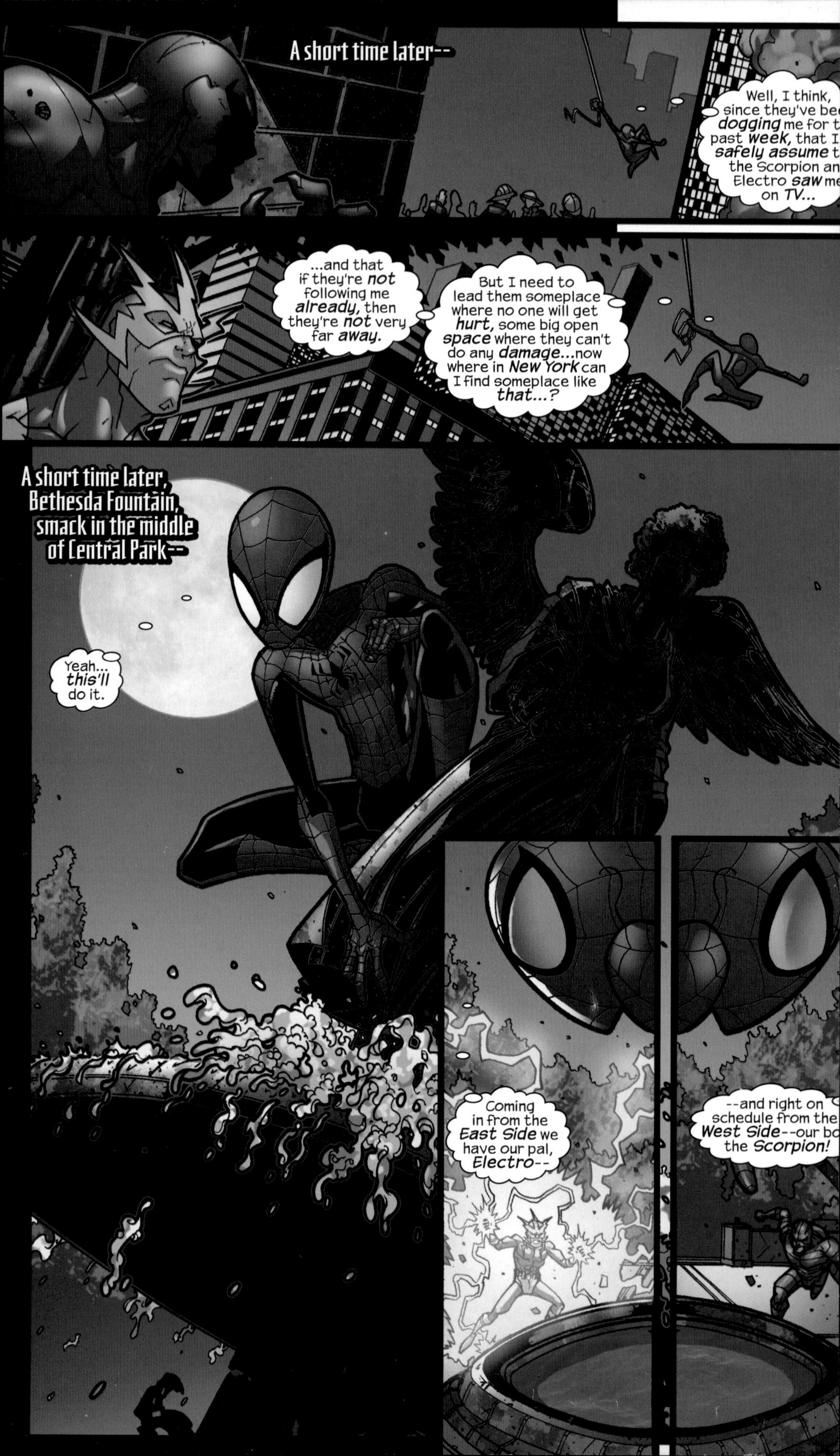

A short time later--
Well, I think, since they've bee dogging me for t past week, that I safely assume t the Scorpion an Electro saw me on TV...
...and that if they're not following me already, then they're not very far away.
But I need to lead them someplace where no one will get hurt, some big open space where they can't do any damage...now where in New York can I find someplace like that...?
A short time later, Bethesda Fountain, smack in the middle of Central Park--
Yeah... this'll do it.
Coming in from the East Side we have our pal, Electro--
--and right on schedule from the West Side--our bo the Scorpion!

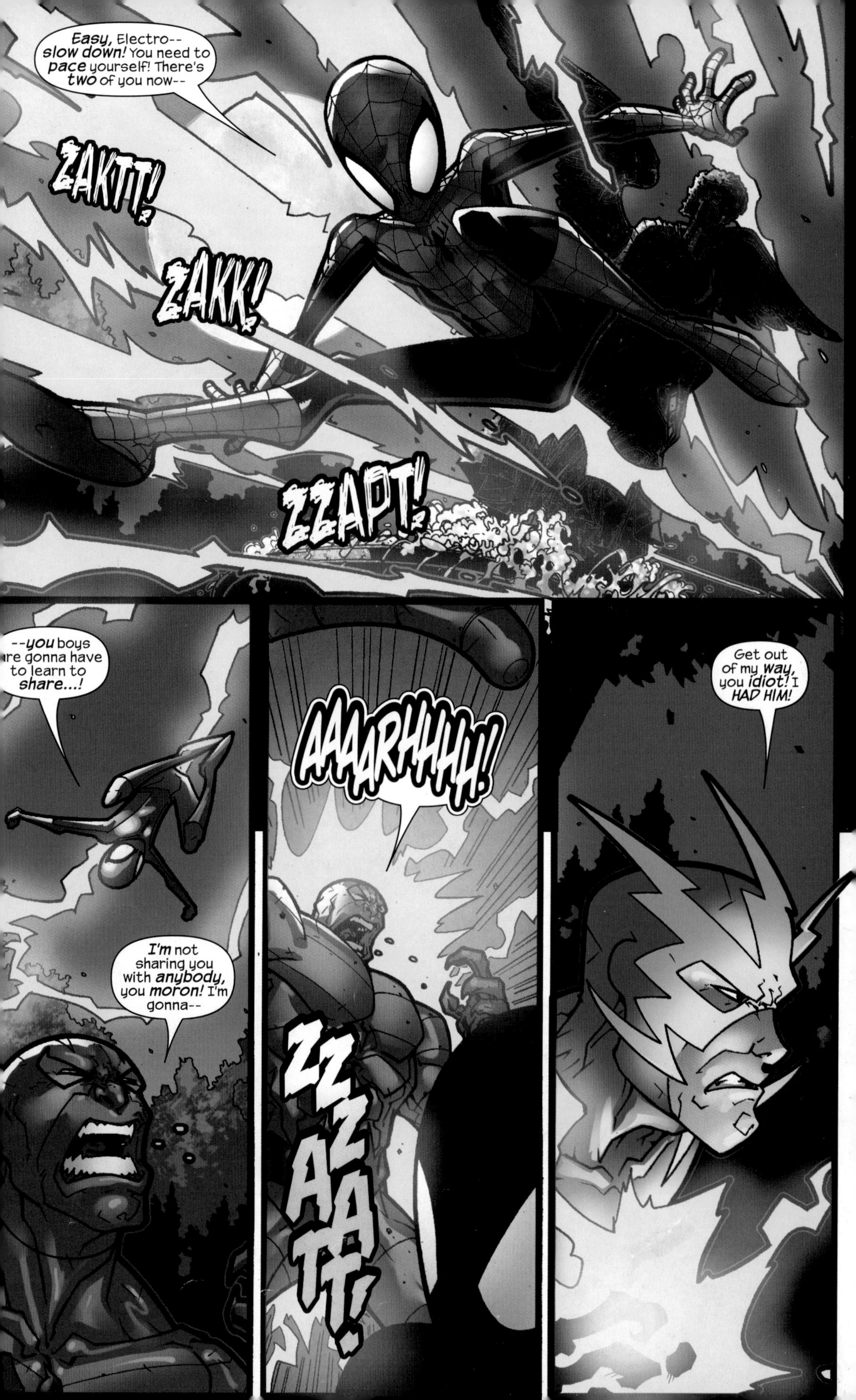
Easy, Electro-- slow down! You need to pace yourself! There's two of you now--
ZAKTT!
ZAKK!
ZZAPT!
--you boys are gonna have to learn to share...!
I'm not sharing you with anybody, you moron! I'm gonna--
AAAARHHHH!
ZZZAATT!
Get out of my way, you idiot! I HAD HIM!

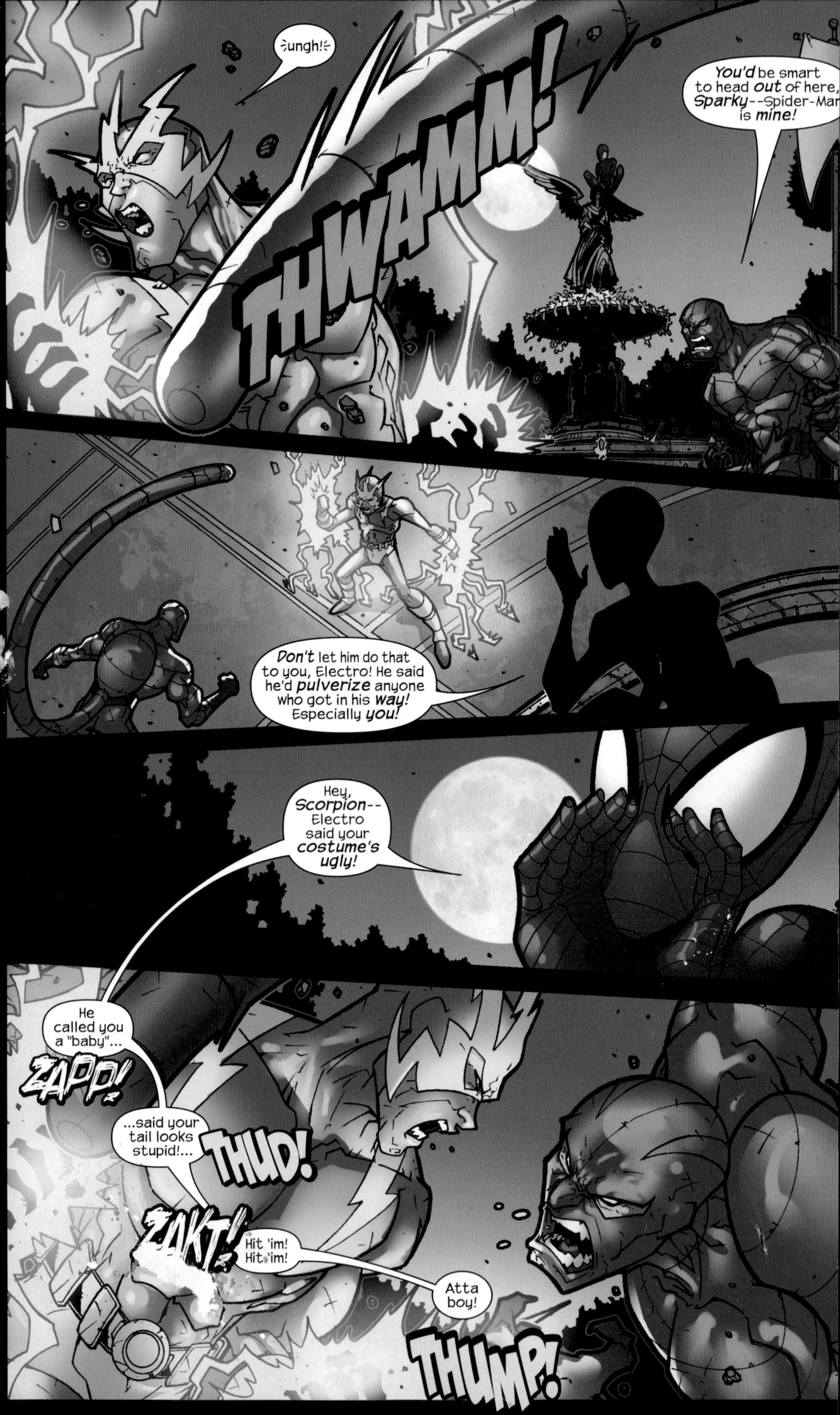

ungh!
THWAMM!
You'd be smart to head out of here, Sparky--Spider-Man is mine!
Don't let him do that to you, Electro! He said he'd pulverize anyone who got in his way! Especially you!
Hey, Scorpion--Electro said your costume's ugly!
He called you a "baby"...
ZAPP!
...said your tail looks stupid!...
THUD!
ZAKT!
Hit 'im! Hit 'im!
Atta boy!
THUMP!

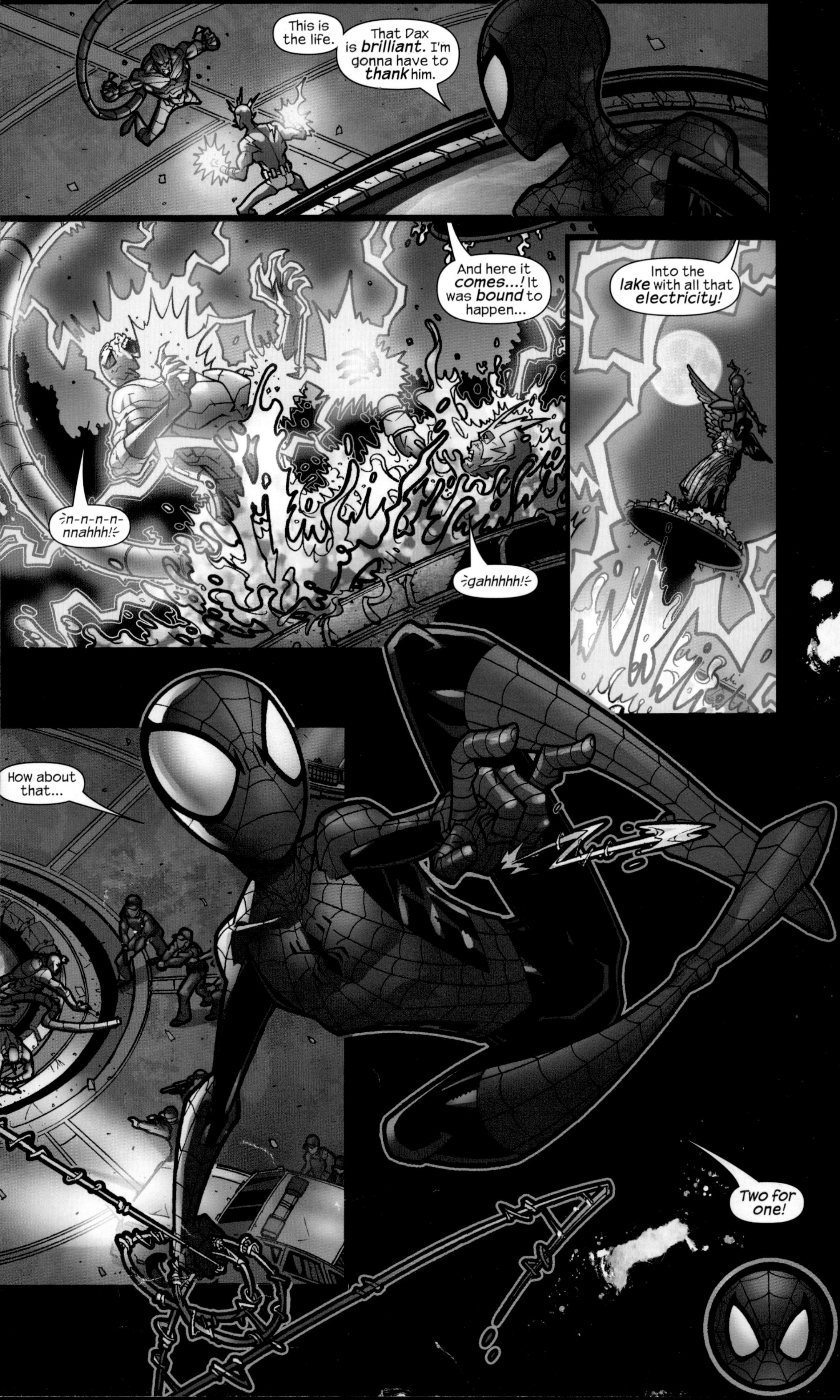
This is the life.
That Dax is **brilliant.** I'm gonna have to ***thank*** him.
And here it ***comes...!*** It was ***bound*** to happen...
n-n-n-n-nnahhh!
gahhhhh!
Into the ***lake*** with all that ***electricity!***
How about that...
Two for one!

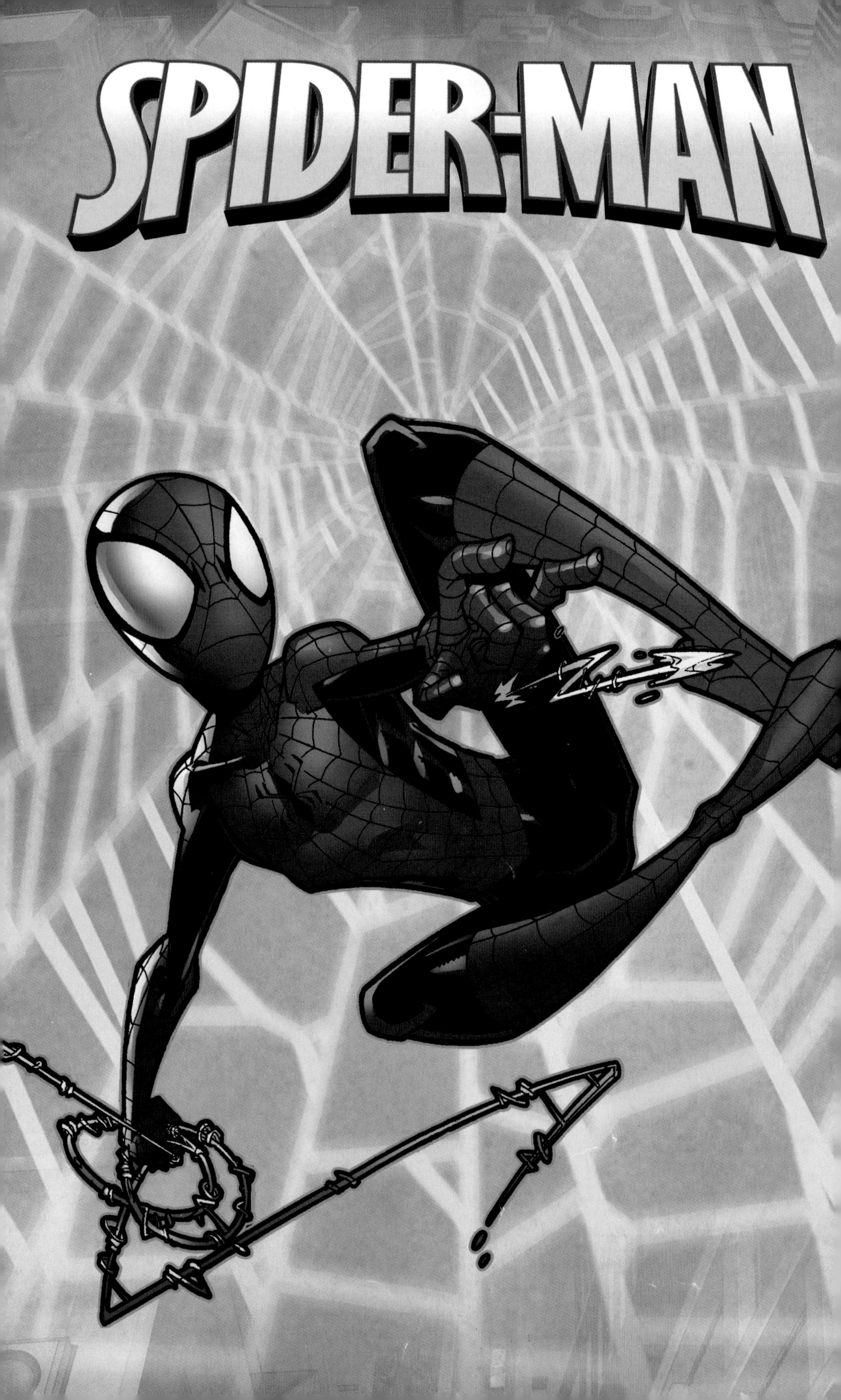
SPIDER-MAN